Kitty
the Tiger
Fairy

Special thanks to
Narinder Dhami

ORCHARD BOOKS
338 Euston Road, London NW1 3BH
Orchard Books Australia
Level 17/207 Kent Street, Sydney, NSW 2000
A Paperback Original

First published in 2013 by Orchard Books

HiT entertainment

A CIP catalogue record for this book is available
from the British Library.

ISBN 978 1 40832 794 4

1 3 5 7 9 10 8 6 4 2

Printed in Great Britain

The paper and board used in this paperback are natural recyclable
products made from wood grown in sustainable forests. The
manufacturing processes conform to the environmental regulations
of the country of origin.

Orchard Books is a division of Hachette Children's Books,
an Hachette UK company

www.hachette.co.uk

Kitty
the Tiger
Fairy

by Daisy Meadows

ORCHARD

www.rainbowmagic.co.uk

The Fairyland Palace

Meadow

Stream

Beehive

Arctic Tundra

Eucalyptus Forest

Tropical Waterfall

Jack Frost's
Ice Castle

To Jack Frost's Zoo

Wild Woods
Nature
Reserve

Watering Hole

Pagoda

Desert Oasis

Jack Frost's Spell

I love animals, yes I do,
I want my very own private zoo!
I'll capture the animals one by one,
With fairy magic to help me on!

A koala, a tiger, an Arctic fox,
I'll keep them in cages with giant locks.
Every kind of animal will be there,
A panda, a meerkat, a honey bear.
The animals will be my property,
I'll be master of a huge menagerie!

Contents

Return to Wild Woods

"I can't wait to find out what we'll be doing today!" Rachel Walker exclaimed eagerly as she followed her best friend, Kirsty Tate, through Wild Woods Nature Reserve. "I hope we see lots of different animals."

It was the school summer holidays, and the girls' parents had arranged for them to spend a week as junior rangers at

Kirsty's local nature reserve. The reserve was a haven for all kinds of animals like hares, otters and red squirrels.

"We'll have loads of lovely photos to remind us of our time here at Wild Woods," Kirsty remarked as the girls wound their way through the trees, carrying their backpacks. She stopped to snap a red-and-blue butterfly drinking nectar from a drift of wildflowers and then showed the photo to Rachel.

"It's beautiful," Rachel said admiringly. "Look, Kirsty, there's Becky with the other junior rangers."

She pointed to the clearing ahead of them where a group of girls and boys were gathered around the head of the nature reserve. "I bet she's got some interesting jobs for us!"

Becky was chatting with a couple of the junior rangers. She spotted the girls and waved at them.

"Everyone's here now, so good morning to you all," Becky announced with a huge smile. "I'm thrilled you're back for more important wildlife work here at Wild Woods Nature Reserve! Did you enjoy yourselves yesterday?"

"YES!" everyone shouted, full of excitement.

"Well, we have a very busy day ahead of us," she informed them. "I have a special job for you down at the stream. So you can start off by getting yourselves dressed up in *these*!" Becky pointed to a pile of long rubber Wellington boots heaped on the grass beside her. Rachel

and Kirsty queued up with the other junior rangers to collect a pair each, and then they pulled the rubber boots on. The wellies were so long, they covered their legs right up to their thighs.

"I feel like Puss-in-Boots!" Kirsty murmured to Rachel with a grin.

Becky grabbed a rake that was leaning against a nearby tree and a net lying on the grass. "Follow me, everyone," she called, walking off through the woods.

"I wonder why we're going to the stream?" Rachel remarked as everyone set off after Becky. "I hope we'll be able to do the special job, whatever it is."

"If we finish it, we might get another badge," Kirsty said hopefully. Becky had given the girls badges with a picture of a tree on them after they'd successfully managed to plant some young saplings the day before. Rachel and Kirsty had proudly pinned the badges to their backpacks. "And maybe..." Kirsty lowered her voice so that no-one else could hear, "our fairy friends will need our help again today, too!"

When the girls had arrived at the nature reserve yesterday, they'd been thrilled to see their friend Bertram, the frog footman from Fairyland. Bertram was visiting relatives who lived in a pond in Wild Woods, and he'd offered to take the girls to the Fairyland Nature Reserve. Of course, Rachel and Kirsty had agreed immediately. They'd been taken on a tour of the Fairyland Reserve by their old friend Fluffy the squirrel, and they'd seen lots of fascinating animals there, like penguins in the ice and snow, and monkeys swinging through the jungle. The girls had also met the seven Baby Animal Rescue Fairies whose job it was to look after the Fairyland Nature Reserve and to protect wildlife everywhere, in both the fairy and human worlds.

Rachel and Kirsty had been having a wonderful time with their fairy friends until Jack Frost turned up and ruined everything! Jack Frost had declared loudly that he liked animals so much, he was going to collect one of each kind for his private zoo. Then, with a magical ice bolt, he stole the Baby Animal Rescue Fairies' charms — the tiny, furry animal key rings that helped them to care for wildlife. Jack Frost had given the key rings to his goblins, ordering them to hurry away to the human world and bring him some animals for his zoo!

"We'll be on the look-out for goblins as well as wildlife," Rachel whispered. The girls had promised to help the Baby Animal Rescue Fairies retrieve their magical key rings, as well as protect the animals that selfish Jack Frost wanted to capture for his private zoo. The fairies had been very grateful. All seven of them had waved their wands together, and their combined magic had gifted Rachel and Kirsty the power to talk to animals.

"It was very naughty of the goblins to kidnap Pan Pan the baby panda yesterday," Kirsty recalled as Becky led them deeper into the woods. "Still, at least we managed to rescue him and take him back to his mother. Wasn't it amazing talking to a real, live panda, Rachel?"

"Brilliant!" Rachel agreed. "Pan Pan was so cute!" She glanced around. "I can hear water trickling, Kirsty. We must be close to the stream."

Becky led the junior rangers past a clump of oak trees towards the stream. But what the girls saw ahead of them made them come to a dead stop

and gasp in horror.

"Oh no!" Kirsty cried. "What's
happened to the stream?"

Kitty Comes for Help

Everyone could see that the little stream was a complete mess. There was an untidy pile of dead leaves, twigs and overgrown reeds in one section that had created a dam, blocking the flow of water. When the water reached the dam, it had nowhere to go so the stream was overflowing its banks, making the ground underfoot damp and soggy. But below the dam there was barely a trickle of water, and the girls could see the dry stone bed of the stream.

"This is really bad for the wildlife in and around the water here," Becky explained, frowning. "We *must* get the stream flowing freely again." She turned to Rachel and Kirsty. "I'd like you two to do this job, please."

"Okay," the girls agreed eagerly.

"One of you can clear this mess," Becky went on. She began pulling at the dam with the rake, dislodging bits of twigs and leaves. "Then the other can use the net to scoop the stuff out of the water." Becky handed the rake to Kirsty and showed Rachel how to drag the net across the surface of the water, collecting all the rubbish. "Can you do that?"

The girls nodded.

"Excellent!" Becky flashed them a smile. "I'll come back when I've shown the others their jobs further up the stream. Just pile up all the stuff you scoop out on the bank, girls. We can make compost with it. We try to be as green as we can here at Wild Woods!"

"No problem," Rachel called as Becky and the other junior rangers left.

The girls set to work. Kirsty raked out the dam and Rachel tried to catch every single bit of rubbish in her net, and remove it from the water. It was tiring work, but they were determined to get the stream flowing freely again.

Suddenly the flapping of wings overhead made both girls look up. Rachel gasped as she saw a large bird with grey, white and black feathers flying towards them.

"Oh, it's a heron!" Rachel exclaimed.

"Isn't she beautiful?" Kirsty breathed, her eyes wide.

"Thank you for cleaning up the stream," the heron called to them in a high, sweet voice. "I'm looking forward to fishing downstream once the water is flowing again."

"You're welcome," Kirsty called. She and Rachel waved as the heron flew off over the treetops.

"Being able to talk to animals is the best fun!" Rachel said happily as they got back to work.

A few moments later, Rachel heard a rustling among the reeds. She glanced over and saw three pairs of bright, dark eyes watching her. Rachel smiled when she realised that it was a mother otter with her two babies, and she pointed them out to Kirsty.

"Hello there," Kirsty said to the otters.
"Can we help you?"

"I was hoping to teach my babies
to swim," the mother otter explained,
twitching her whiskers. "But the stream
is too deep on one side of this dam and
too shallow on the other."

"We're clearing away the dam," Kirsty
told her. "Why don't you come back a
little later?"

"Good idea," the mother otter agreed. "Thank you!" And the three otters scampered away.

The girls continued pulling the dam apart. More water was beginning to trickle through here and there, which encouraged them to carry on.

"See that big log?" Rachel panted, pointing it out to Kirsty. "I think that's stopping a lot of water getting through. Let's try and pull it out."

Kirsty pulled at the log with her rake, but it didn't budge, even though she put all her weight behind it. Rachel threw the net down and went to help her, but even between them, they couldn't move the log at all. It was stuck fast. Both girls tried and tried, but they were out of breath now, puffing and panting.

"Let's take a break," Kirsty gasped.

There was nowhere to sit down except on the wet ground, so the girls leaned against a nearby tree and rested for a few moments.

"I think we need an energy boost!" Rachel said with a grin. "I've got some cereal bars we can have."

Rachel opened her backpack and took out her tiger-print lunchbox. As she took the lid off, the girls were surprised to see a magical golden glow coming from inside. Then they saw a little fairy dance out of the lunchbox and hover, smiling, in the air before them.

"Kitty the Tiger Fairy!" Kirsty exclaimed excitedly.

Tiger Talk

"Hi, girls!" Kitty said. She was dressed in a striped vest top with rolled-up jeans and fur-trimmed ankle boots. She also wore a headband with tiger ears on top of her blonde curls. "I'm sure you can guess why I'm here."

"Jack Frost's goblins are trying to catch more animals?" Rachel guessed.

Kitty nodded. "Right now those naughty goblins are chasing three tiger cubs, hoping to capture one for Jack Frost's zoo," she replied, frowning anxiously. "And I can't protect the cubs with my magic because the goblins have my magic key ring."

"Can we help?" Kirsty offered eagerly.

Kitty smiled. "Thank you, girls," she replied. "Let's go and stop those dreadful goblins kidnapping my beautiful tigers!"

Kitty shook her wand, conjuring up a cloud of glittering fairy dust. The girls were whisked gently away and in the blink of an eye, Rachel and Kirsty found themselves thousands of miles from the nature reserve. They landed in a beautiful, faraway jungle where they could feel the heat of the red-gold sun overhead. They were standing on a rock jutting out over a river that flowed down from a beautiful, high waterfall. The banks of the river were lined with tall trees and tropical flowers.

"I wonder what's happened to my poor little tiger cubs?" Kitty said anxiously.

Before Rachel or Kirsty could say anything, they heard a loud roar coming from among the trees.

"GO AWAY!"

"Who's that?" Rachel asked curiously. She and Kirsty turned to look. Suddenly the girls saw two tiger cubs slip out from behind a tree and prowl towards them, looking ready to pounce!

Immediately Kitty swooped down lower. "Don't worry, little ones," she called to the tiger cubs. "These are my friends. You're quite safe."

The tiger cubs stopped, looking uncertainly at the girls.

"They're not green like the others!" the biggest cub growled.

"We're not green because we're girls, not goblins," Rachel explained gently.

"And we want to help you, not hurt you," Kirsty added.

The tiger cubs looked much happier.

"Let me introduce you properly," Kitty said with a smile. "Cubs, these are my friends Rachel and Kirsty. Girls, this is Stripes —" she pointed her wand at the biggest cub "— and this is Tig, his brother."

"Pleased to meet you!" Stripes and Tig chorused in their cute, growly little cub voices.

"But, boys, where's your sister, Sheba?" Kitty went on, looking worried. "You three are *always* together."

"We got separated when the little green boys started chasing us," Stripes replied, looking worried.

"We've been looking for Sheba for ages," Tig explained. "We followed her scent to the river, but it finishes here."

"Sheba must have managed to get

across to the other side of the river,"
Kitty guessed.

"Tig and I were going to swim over
and look for her," said Stripes, "but then
we hid in the trees because we thought
you were coming to catch us!"

"We'll help you search for Sheba,"
Rachel offered.

"Thank you," Tig said gratefully.
"We'd offer you a ride on our backs if
you were a little bit smaller."

"Well, that's one problem easily
solved!" Kitty laughed.
With a flick of her
wand, she scattered
magical sparkles
around the girls,
shrinking them both
down into fairies.

Full of excitement, Rachel and Kirsty flew over to the tiger cubs. Kirsty floated down onto Stripes' back and Rachel landed on Tig. *The cubs' fur is as thick, soft and warm as a blanket,* Rachel thought as she stroked Tig's head.

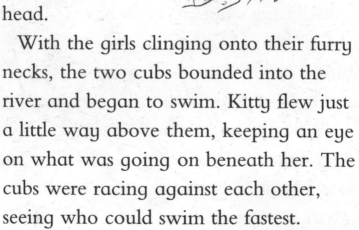

With the girls clinging onto their furry necks, the two cubs bounded into the river and began to swim. Kitty flew just a little way above them, keeping an eye on what was going on beneath her. The cubs were racing against each other, seeing who could swim the fastest.

Tig playfully splashed Stripes with his little paw, and Rachel and Kirsty burst out laughing.

"Hey, stop that!" Stripes growled. He scooped up some water in his paw and tossed it at his brother. A few drops flew upwards and splashed Kitty's clothes as she zoomed along above them.

"Sorry, Kitty!" Stripes called.

"Just keep swimming!" Kitty told him with a smile.

When the tiger cubs reached the other side of the river, they waded out of the water onto the bank. Rachel and Kirsty fluttered off their backs and the cubs shook themselves vigorously to dry their wet fur. Then the two of them were off, noses to the ground, trying to pick up their sister's scent.

"Sheba's been here!" Tig announced, his tail twitching with excitement.

"We can smell her." He and Tig began sniffing their way along the trail Sheba had left. Kitty, Rachel and Kirsty flew after them, following the tiger cubs along the riverbank towards the waterfall.

"I can't see Sheba anywhere," Kitty murmured.

"Maybe she's hiding if she's frightened of the goblins," Rachel suggested.

Suddenly Stripes and Tig stopped, pricking up their ears.

"We can hear something!" Stripes told Kitty and the girls.

Kitty beckoned to Rachel and Kirsty. Silently the three of them flew ahead of the cubs and they heard the faint sound of rough, gruff voices.

"It sounds like goblins!" Kirsty whispered.

Tree Goblins!

Kitty, Rachel and Kirsty wound their way through the lush green jungle towards the sound of the voices. After a few moments, Rachel spotted three goblins climbing up the trunk of a tree ahead of them.

"There they are!" Rachel murmured, pointing them out to Kitty and Kirsty.

"Let's fly higher up the same tree,"
Kitty suggested. "Then we can listen to
what they're saying. We may be able to
find out where Sheba is, as well as my
key ring!"

Keeping high up in the air so that the
goblins wouldn't spot them, Kitty led the
way over to the tree. She floated down
onto one of the higher
branches and Rachel
and Kirsty landed
beside her.

Kirsty peered
through the leaves.
She could see the three
goblins below them. They weren't very
good climbers at all, and they were
huffing and puffing as they tried to move
up from branch to branch.

"This is all your fault!" the goblin who was highest up the tree screeched at the one just below him. "It was *you* who lost the fairy's magical tiger key ring!"

"Lost!" Kitty repeated under her breath, looking dismayed.

"It really wasn't *my* fault," the second goblin whined.

The third goblin was even lower down the tree and was struggling to swing himself up to the next branch. He made a giant, desperate lunge and ended up hanging upside-down from the branch by his legs, like a bat.

Kitty and the girls tried hard not to laugh at him.

"I need help!" the goblin shrieked.

The first and second goblins ignored him and carried on arguing.

"*You* were carrying the fairy's magic key ring," the first goblin shouted accusingly. "And now you don't have it – so it *must* be your fault!"

The second goblin looked rather sheepish. "I wasn't expecting those tiger cubs to be so scary," he mumbled. "And anyway, the magical key ring isn't *really* lost – we know where it is. The smallest tiger cub has it."

Kitty glanced excitedly at the girls. "That's Sheba!" she whispered.

Suddenly there was a rustling in the undergrowth down below. The next moment, Stripes and Tig burst out and raced towards the tree, growling fiercely. The girls could understand what the cubs were roaring. *Where's our sister?*

The goblins were terrified. Two of them hauled the third up to join them, and they all sat shivering and shaking on the branch below Kitty and the girls.

"I have an idea how to find Sheba as well as Kitty's magic key ring!" Rachel murmured, her face lighting up.

Quickly she outlined her plan to Kitty and Kirsty, then the two girls flew down to the goblins.

"Oh no!" shouted the first goblin. "Pesky fairies *and* scary tiger cubs!"

"Make them go away!" the second goblin yelled at the girls, pointing down at Stripes and Tig who were growling loudly.

"We can understand tiger talk," Rachel said. "They're asking you where their sister is."

The three goblins glanced at each other. "We're not telling you!" the third goblin snapped rudely. Then he wobbled a little on the branch and gave a shriek of fright. "Tell them! Tell them!" he shouted at the others. "Otherwise we'll be stuck here for ever or we'll fall out of the tree and the tigers will get us!"

"We saw her going up to the top of the big waterfall," the first goblin mumbled sulkily.

"But then we lost sight of her," the second goblin added.

Kitty, who had been listening above them, quickly swooped down to Stripes and Tig.

"The goblins don't have Sheba," she told the cubs. "She's somewhere at the top of the waterfall. Let them go."

Obediently the tiger cubs stopped growling and sat down on the grass.

In the meantime, the three silly goblins shinned down the tree as fast as they could and ran off without a backward glance.

"Meet you at the top of the waterfall," Stripes shouted to Kitty and the girls. "Come on, Tig!" And the cubs ran towards the cliff as fast as they could in a blur of orange and black.

Kitty, Rachel and Kirsty flew to the river and followed it to the pool at the bottom of the waterfall. Then they fluttered upwards, enjoying the cool, fresh air and the sight of the clear, sparkling water tumbling down over the cliff face. Kirsty laughed as she flew a little too close and droplets of water landed onto her face.

"Isn't it beautiful?" she sighed.

"Gorgeous," Rachel agreed, turning

to look at the view of the river winding along below them.

Kirsty glanced up and saw Stripes and Tig waiting for them on top of the cliff.

But all of a sudden she saw another flash of orange-and-black *behind* the cascading waterfall.

"Is that you, Sheba?" Kirsty called.

Sheba's Splashing

Kirsty turned to Rachel and Kitty.
"I think I just saw Sheba the tiger cub
behind the waterfall!" she told them
breathlessly.

"Let's go and see," Kitty said
immediately. "I'm afraid we'll get rather
wet, though." She linked hands with
Rachel and Kirsty. "Get ready, girls!"

Kirsty took a deep breath. They were about to get very, very wet. She just hoped it *was* Sheba that she'd seen!

Swiftly, the three friends zoomed around the falling sheet of water and landed on a ledge behind it. Now they could see the cliff face right in front of them.

"Look, there's a little cave just there," Rachel said, smoothing back her wet

hair. "I wonder if Sheba's inside?"

They peered into the cave. To Kirsty's delight, she saw a little tiger cub rolling around on the ground. She was playing with a tiger key ring, throwing it into the air and catching it between her paws. Kirsty could see the key ring was surrounded by a faint, golden glow that lit up the dark cave.

"My magical key ring!" Kitty murmured. "Hello, Sheba. You can come out of the cave now. The goblins have gone."

"Don't want to!" Sheba growled cheekily, her green eyes full of mischief. "I'm having too much fun!"

"Animals love our special key rings," Kitty reminded the girls, as Sheba continued batting the furry tiger around. "She won't give it up easily! But if we can find something else Sheba likes, then she might forget about my key ring."

"I'll see what I've got," said Rachel, beginning to rummage in her pocket.

"Wait, remember how much Stripes and Tig enjoyed playing around in the water?" Kirsty said slowly. "Maybe Sheba would come out if she thought she was missing a whole lot of fun?"

"That's a great idea," Kitty agreed.

Kirsty peeped into the cave again. "It's time for a little tiger to splash about in

the river!" she said. "Come on, Sheba,
you don't want to miss all the fun."

Sheba's eyes lit up. "Hurrah!" she cried
in her growly voice, dropping Kitty's
tiger on the ground. She batted it across
the cave to Kirsty with her paw
and then she ran out, and jumped
straight through the waterfall

into the pool not far
below them.

"Thank
goodness!"
Kitty
murmured
gratefully
as she rushed
over to retrieve
her magical charm.
The instant she touched it, the key ring
shrank down to its Fairyland size and
Kitty clipped it firmly to the waistband
of her jeans.

As Kitty and the girls flew around the
waterfall once more, they could hear
splashing and yelps of delight below
them. Stripes and Tig had spotted Sheba
in the pool and rushed down from the

cliff to join her. The three cubs were
having a water fight!

Suddenly Rachel saw the three goblins
rush out from the trees. "Be careful,
cubs!" she yelled. "Here come the mean
goblins again!"

"We need a tiger for Jack Frost's zoo!"
the first goblin shouted. "Grab them!"

"GO AWAY!" Stripes, Tig and Sheba
roared in unison. The three goblins
shrieked in terror and huddled together

on the riverbank, their teeth chattering with fright.

"You can't just take any animals you want, whatever Jack Frost says," Kitty said sternly as she, Rachel and Kirsty swooped down towards the goblins.

"Animals aren't objects to be collected, you know!" Rachel added.

Then Kirsty gave a gasp of surprise. She'd just spotted a large, fully grown tiger standing on the rock jutting out over the river.

"Look at that enormous tiger over there!" Kirsty exclaimed nervously. "It looks really fierce…"

Going with the Flow

This was too much for the goblins. They fled immediately, falling over their own big feet to get away as fast as they could.

"It's the cubs' mother," Kitty explained. "Come and say hello." She led the girls over to the tiger. "These are my friends, Rachel and Kirsty," Kitty told her.

"Hello, girls," the mother tiger purred in a gentle voice. "Thank you for finding my cubs. I was extremely worried about them."

"Mother! Mother!" the cubs chorused, and they began paddling across the pool towards her.

"And thank you, Rachel and Kirsty, for finding my magic tiger key ring." Kitty patted the key ring attached to her jeans. "I'll be off to Fairyland now to tell them the good news!"

An idea popped into Kirsty's head.

"Before you go, Kitty, could you help us out at Wild Woods?" she asked.

"Of course!" Kitty said instantly.

They all called goodbye to the mother tiger, Stripes, Tig and Sheba. Then Kitty's magic restored the girls to their normal size and whirled them off to Wild Woods Nature Reserve. Just a few seconds later, the three of them were back at the stream.

"We can't move that log," Kirsty explained, pointing it out to Kitty. "Can you help?"

"I certainly can," Kitty agreed, smiling. She tapped the log with her wand, showering it with fairy dust. The log immediately rose up out of the water, floated through the air and came to rest on the bank of the stream.

"Thank you, Kitty," Kirsty said happily. "Look, Rachel, the water's starting to flow again!"

The girls cheered as the water splashed through the gap left by the big heavy log and began to fill up the dry bed of the stream.

"And now I really must go," Kitty smiled. "Goodbye, girls. I know I can count on you to help protect wildlife *everywhere* from Jack Frost and his naughty goblins!" And she vanished in a puff of glittery fairy dust.

Then the girls heard the sound of beating wings overhead and the heron swooped down to land on the bank beside them.

"The water's flowing again!" the heron said excitedly. "Now I can fish downstream whenever I like."

Rachel nudged Kirsty. "And here come the three otters!" she said.

The mother otter was leading her two babies to the edge of the water. "Hello, girls," she called to Rachel and Kirsty.

69

Then she turned to her babies. "Just do what I do," she told them, and slipped into the water. Her babies followed, looking rather nervous.

"You're doing really well!" Kirsty called, and she and Rachel applauded as the baby otters paddled hesitantly across the stream.

Suddenly the girls heard the sound of footsteps and they saw Becky approaching through the trees. The

heron flew away and the otters swam
into a clump of reeds to hide.

"How are you getting on, girls?" Becky
asked. Then she gave an exclamation of
delight. "You've got the stream flowing
again – that's wonderful!" Then she
noticed the log on the bank. "How on
earth did you manage to move that?
Very well done! It'll be a perfect bench
for visitors."

Rachel and Kirsty grinned at each other.

"I think you both deserve a second badge," Becky went on, handing one to Rachel and another to Kirsty. "As you can see, these badges have a picture of the river on them."

The girls were thrilled.

"And I have another tricky task for you tomorrow," Becky went on, her eyes twinkling.

"Do you think you'll be able to do it?"

"We hope so!" Rachel replied with a grin.

"A tricky task?" Kirsty whispered as Becky went off to check on the other junior rangers. "It *can't* be trickier than helping the Baby Animal Rescue Fairies protect wildlife from Jack Frost!"

"True," Rachel whispered back. "We'd better be ready for anything!"

"So, all we know about today's job is
that it's going to be particularly tricky!"
Kirsty Tate remarked to her best friend,
Rachel Walker, as they wound their way
along a path through the woods.

The two girls had volunteered to spend
a week of the summer holidays working
as junior rangers at Wild Woods Nature
Reserve. "What do you think we'll be
doing, Rachel?"

"I don't know, but I'm looking forward
to finding out when we meet Becky in
the meadow!" Rachel replied with a
grin. Becky was the head of the nature

reserve. "I hope it's something we can do really well — and then we *might* just get another badge."

"I *love* getting badges," Kirsty said happily. She swung her backpack off her shoulders so she could proudly sneak a peek at the badges pinned to the pockets. This was the girls' third day at Wild Woods and they'd won the badges because they'd managed to complete their tasks successfully on the previous two days.

Read **Mara the Meerkat Fairy** to find out what adventures are in store for Kirsty and Rachel!

Meet the
Baby Animal Rescue
Fairies

The Baby Animal Rescue Fairies have lost all their magical items. But luckily, Kirsty and Rachel are there to save the day and make sure all baby animals in the world are safe and sound.

www.rainbowmagicbooks.co.uk

Look out for the next sparkly
Rainbow Magic Special!

Robyn the
Christmas Party Fairy

Rachel and Kirsty are helping to organise a big Christmas party.
But Jack Frost has stolen Robyn the Christmas Party Fairy's
magical objects! The girls must help Robyn, before the spirit
of Christmas is lost forever...

Out now!

Meet the fairies, play games
and get sneak peeks at
the latest books!

www.rainbowmagicbooks.co.uk

There's fairy fun for everyone on
our wonderful website.
You'll find great activities, competitions, stories and
fairy profiles, and also a special newsletter.

Competition!

The Baby Animal Rescue Fairies have created
a special competition just for you!
In the back of each book in the series there will be
a question for you to answer.
Once you have collected all the books and all
seven answers, go online and enter the competition!

We will put all the correct entries into a draw and select
a winner to receive a special Rainbow Magic Goody Bag,
featuring lots of treats for you and your fairy friends.
The winner will also star in a new Rainbow Magic story!

Who was the first Rainbow Magic Fairy?

— — — —

Enter online now at www.rainbowmagicbooks.co.uk

No purchase required. Only one entry per child.
Two prize draws will take place on 1st April 2014 and 2nd July 2014. Alternatively readers can
send the answer on a postcard to: Rainbow Magic, Baby Animal Rescue Fairies Competition,
Orchard Books, 338 Euston Road, London, NW1 3BH. Australian readers can write to:
Rainbow Magic, Baby Animal Rescue Fairies Competition, Hachette Children's Books,
level 17/207 Kent St, Sydney, NSW 2000. E-mail: childrens.books@hachette.com.au.
New Zealand readers should write to:
Rainbow Magic, Baby Animal Rescue Fairies Competition,
4 Whetu Place, Mairangi Bay, Auckland, NZ

Meet the
Rainbow Fairies

Also available as an ebook

Collect the seven original Rainbow Fairies
to find out how the adventure began!

www.rainbowmagicbooks.co.uk